For my brother, Frazer,
who makes things and mends them – S.H.

To Embla & Eirik – X.L.

Farshore

First published in Great Britain 2021 by Farshore
An imprint of HarperCollins*Publishers*
1 London Bridge Street, London SE1 9GF
www.farshore.co.uk

HarperCollins*Publishers*
1st Floor, Watermarque Building, Ringsend Road
Dublin 4, Ireland

Text copyright © Sam Hay 2021
Illustrations copyright © Xin Li 2021

Sam Hay and Xin Li have asserted their moral rights.

ISBN 978 1 4052 9821 6
Printed in China.
1

A CIP catalogue record for this title is available from the British Library.

Stay safe online. Farshore is not responsible for content hosted by third parties.

Farshore takes its responsibility to the planet and its inhabitants very seriously.
We aim to use papers from well-managed forests run by responsible suppliers.

The Star Maker's Apprentice

Sam Hay & Xin Li

Farshore

Finn's father had a very special job.
He made stars. And mended them.
It was busy work, for stars were easily broken . . .

They got bumped.
And **biffed**.
And squashed.
And **squished**.
They got frozen.
Or **shattered**.
Or blown away
all together.

Finn longed to help his father. He had lots of **dazzling ideas** to make the stars look even more special.

But his father wasn't so sure. "People don't like things that are different!" he said firmly. So Finn put his ideas back in his art box.

Then one shivery winter's night,
Finn's father didn't look so good.
His head hurt and he couldn't
stop **achoo-ing!**

"I'll make the stars for you,"
offered Finn.
"And mend them!"

But his father shook
his head.

"The tools are too sharp.
The sparkle glue is too sticky and
the star machine doesn't always
do what it's meant to."

Then he fell asleep
with a sigh.

But Finn couldn't resist
taking just a tiny peek . . .

The tools **were** a bit sharp.

The sparkle glue **did** look a bit sticky.

But the star machine didn't look difficult.

Nope, not at all.

And Finn **really** wanted to help his father.

So, he opened the lid and
poured in a sack of stardust,
a bag of brightness, and
a drop of twinkle ink.

He pressed the
big red button and . . .

bloop!
out popped a star.

Bloop! Bloop!
out popped two more.

But without the sparkle glue,
they looked a bit . . . dull.

Then Finn remembered his
art box and a **colourful
idea** popped into his head.

Inside the box were buttons and ribbons and streamers and pipe cleaners and crayons and glitter – lots of glitter.

Finn tipped it all into the star machine, which began to whirr and thrum.
It shuddered
and juddered and –

BLOOP BLOOP BLO

BLOOP

BLOOP

BLOOP

BLOOP

BLOOP

BLOOP

BLOOP

BLO

This time the stars were different.
Oh yes! This time Finn's stars were
spectacular!

Beaming with pride,
Finn scooped up his
special stars,

and took them outside . . .

and hung them in the sky.

He couldn't wait to show his father
how **beautiful** they looked.

BLOOP
BLOOP
BLOOP

But back in the cabin
on the mountaintop . . .

... the star machine was still whirring and juddering.

And by the time Finn got home –

Oh!

There were spectacular stars
everywhere, pouring out of the
door and windows in a giant,
sparkly wave.

Suddenly with a swoosh,
the wave swept Finn off his feet

and down,
down the mountainside,
faster and faster.

I have to get off,
Finn thought.
But how?

Then he remembered
something special
about stars.

He crossed his
fingers . . .

and made a wish!

"Finn!"

Finn landed safely in his father's arms
just as the starry wave soared into the sky.

As Finn's stars spread across the sky, his father looked in horror.
"Oh, Finn, people don't like things that are different."

But Finn wasn't looking at the sky . . .

He was looking at
the faces of the people, as they
rushed out of their houses, ooh-ing
and ahh-ing, smiling and pointing at
the winking, twinkling, shimmering,
spectacular stars.

Finn's father stared in amazement.

"Perhaps people do
like things that are different,"
he said with a smile.

Of course, it wasn't long
before Finn's new stars got bumped
and biffed. And squashed and squished.
And frozen and shattered.
Some blew away **all together.**

And Finn's father had to make new ones.

But this time,
Finn was allowed to help.
And sometimes, together, they'd
make **Finn's special stars.**

Then **all across the world,**
people would look up in wonder at
the eye-popping, jaw-dropping, extra special,
light-up-the-night, spectacular stars.

And the Star Maker and his apprentice
would twinkle with joy.